WITHDRAWN
No longer the property of the
Boston Public Library.
Sale of this material benefits the Library

The Fashion Kitty Collection

Book One

Fashion Kitty

Book Two

Fashion Kitty versus the Fashion Queen

by Charise Mericle Harper

Disney Hyperion
Los Angeles New York

If you purchased this book without a cover, you should be aware that this book is stolen property. It was reported as "unsold and destroyed" to the publisher, and neither the author nor the publisher has received any payment for this "stripped" book.

Fashion Kitty copyright © 2005 by Charise Mericle Harper

Fashion Kitty versus the Fashion Queen copyright © 2007 by Charise Mericle Harper

All rights reserved. Published by Disney • Hyperion, an imprint of Disney Book Group. No part of this book may be reproduced or transmitted in any form or by any means, electronic or mechanical, including photocopying, recording, or by any information storage and retrieval system, without written permission from the publisher. For information address Disney • Hyperion, 125 West End Avenue, New York, New York 10023.

First Paperback Edition of *Fashion Kitty*, September 2005

First Paperback Edition of *Fashion Kitty versus the Fashion Queen*, June 2007

First Bind-Up Edition, November 2019

10 9 8 7 6 5 4 3 2 1

FAC-029191-19221

Printed in Malaysia

This book is set in Belwe Mono/ITC; Julietrose, Kidprint/Monotype

Designed by Christine Kettner and David Hastings

Library of Congress Control Number for *Fashion Kitty*: 2005040435

Library of Congress Control Number for *Fashion Kitty versus the Fashion Queen* Hardcover: 2007299791

ISBN 978-1-368-04963-4

Visit www.DisneyBooks.com

Book One

Fashion

Kitty

Christine, thanks for making this book
grow from this— to this—

For Alessandra
for believing
in F.K.
For Ivy
for being
such a girl
For Amy-
my friend
and fan of
great shoes
S.M.
L.H.

This is Kiki Kittie.

She lives with her mother, father, little sister, Lana, and pet mouse named Mousie. The Kittie family is unusual for three reasons:

1 The Kittie family has a pet mouse.

2 Kiki and Lana get to pick out all their own clothes.

3 The Kittie family knows the secret identity of Fashion Kitty.

The **FIRST** reason the Kittie family is unusual is that a cat having a mouse for a pet is similar to a human having a chocolate cake for a pet.

Only, the Kittie family doesn't feel that way about Mousie, because they are vegetarians . . .

We love cheese!
And milk,
and ice cream,
and pancakes!

. . . which means they don't eat meat.

But being unusual means that other cats, even the Kittie family's friends and relatives, probably wouldn't feel the same way about Mousie.

Even though the Kittie family loves all their friends, they decided to keep Mousie a secret. After all, every family has a few secrets.

Father Kittie built Mousie a special smell-proof clubhouse in the closet in Kiki's room. Any time cats come over, Mousie runs into the clubhouse and locks the door.

Your house always smells so deliciously cheesy.
Once Mousie is safe in her clubhouse, Mother Kittie sprays blue-cheese air freshener all over the house, just to be safe.
Thank you, Emma.

If Kiki could tell her cat friends about Mousie, she'd say:
Mousie is not her real name.
She's really called Phoebe Frederique. Doesn't that sound glamorous?

But she can't tell anybody Mousie's real name, not even her family, because six months ago . . .

Which was no big surprise because . . .

It's just you and me, Phoebe Frederique!!
Friends forever!
Kiki only whispers Mousie's real name when they are alone.

The second reason the Kittie family is unusual is that Mother Kittie believes in free fashion, which means she lets Kiki and Lana pick out all their own clothes. Most mothers don't do this because it upsets them when patterns like:

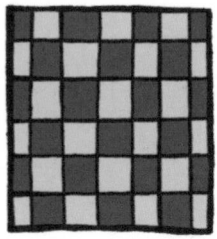

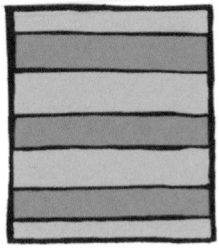

are displayed all together on one body.

This doesn't bother Mother Kittie. As long as Kiki and Lana wear jackets and hats in the wintertime, Mother Kittie is happy.

Kiki has a natural flair for fashion.
Everyone says so:

Lana, on the other hand, is a different story. She wears some very unusual clothing combinations.

Sometimes Kiki just can't help herself and she says:

says Lana, who then runs off to do whatever four-year-olds do.

Kiki is glad that Lana doesn't go to school yet. At least at home no one can see her.

says Mother Kittie when Kiki complains.

But Kiki knows that mothers don't always see the truth about their children, and she secretly wonders if sometimes they are too nice.

The **THIRD** and most important reason the Kittie family is unusual is that they know the secret identity of Fashion Kitty.

Usually this is more of a girl thing than a boy thing, but that is only because many boys don't give two hoots about fashion.

Sometimes that's not a good thing.

Fashion Kitty doesn't live on top of a mountain,

in a fancy apartment building,

or even in a stylish secret superhero cave.

She lives with her mother, father, and little sister, Lana. That's right! Fashion Kitty is really Kiki Kittie. Kiki wasn't always a fashion hero. Right up until her birthday four months ago, Kiki Kittie was just her regular fashionable self. But on her birthday, something unexplainable happened.

Kiki was blowing out her candles on her birthday cake when a shelf above her broke and sent a pile of fashion magazines tumbling down on her head.

In fact, the list of unfortunate things that happened in the next six seconds is quite long.

It was unfortunate that...

the shelf broke when Kiki was directly underneath it blowing out the candles on her birthday cake;

the magazines hit Kiki on the head, causing her to fall down and knock over the table that held the birthday cake;

the falling table pushed Lana onto the floor, headfirst into the birthday cake;

Mother Kittie accidentally kicked Father Kittie on the leg when she tried to catch the falling Lana;

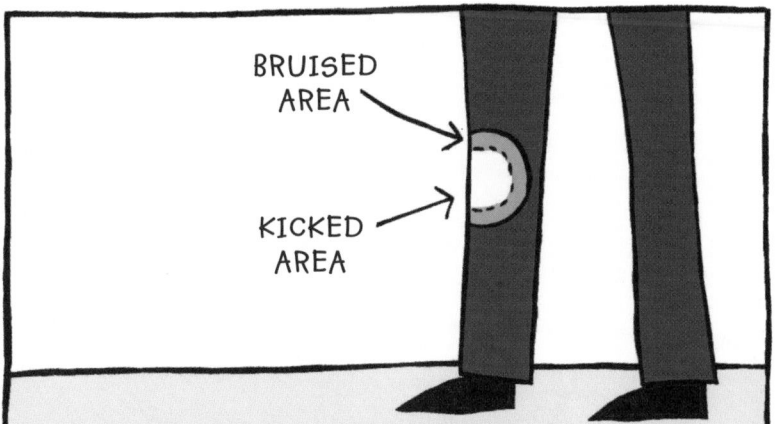

the leg Mother Kittie kicked already had a big bruise on it from two days before, when Father Kittie had tripped on one of Lana's toys;

Father Kittie, while yelling and grabbing his sore leg, knocked over a prized antique vase that was his and Mrs. Kittie's favorite wedding present;

and the vase broke.

But the most unfortunate thing was that Kiki Kittie was lying very still on the floor, with her eyes closed, and she was not sleeping.

Often, when bad things happen, it is comforting to make a silent list of how it could have been worse.

Looking at the mess, Mother Kittie said:

And then they laughed, because Lana was covered with chocolate cake.

Later, when everything was almost cleaned up and everyone was getting ready to go out to Tom's Treats, the most fancy and delicious cake-and-ice-cream restaurant in town, Lana said:

And everyone agreed it was.

And then, right when everything seemed almost normal, the unexplainable thing happened. Kiki screamed and fell to the floor. Mother and Father Kittie rushed over, thinking the same horrible thought:

In fact, Kiki was just fine, except that she wasn't Kiki anymore. When she stood up she was . . .

Fashion

Kitty

I hear a call of despair.

Not far away, but in desperate need of help.

May I borrow those stockings from your stylish outfit?
Uh, Okay

This will have to be my mask for now.
I'll make something better later.

said Fashion Kitty, and she flew out the door, leaving Mother and Father Kittie, Lana, and even Mousie standing there with their mouths open.

Super Abilities of Fashion Kitty
Brain that can mix and match hundreds of outfits in a second
Ears that hear the distress call of someone in need of fashion help
X-ray eyes that can see through buildings or anything else that's in the way
Heart, mostly good
Tail of comfort. One touch of the tail makes everything seem all right
Supersonic feet that make Fashion Kitty really bounce

Fashion Kitty flew swiftly through the night sky.
Someone is about to make a fashion faux pas.*
* means big mistake

She knew exactly where the signal was coming from.
It's not their fault.
I must SAVE them!

She flew down to a house, hopped in the window, and landed on the carpet in front of a very startled Mary Jane Tabby.
EEEKK!
Have no fear. I'm Fashion Kitty, and I'm here to help you with your fashion faux pas.
Please don't hurt me. I don't have your fashion faux pas!

Fashion Kitty had to explain herself again. When you are just starting out as a fashion hero, things aren't so easy.
NO! Faux pas means big mistake. I'm here to help you. If you wear that outfit to school tomorrow, it will be a big mistake!
But Priscilla Persian, the most popular kitty in school, gave me a secret note that said all her friends were going to wear polka-dotted shorts over their pants tomorrow.
She's never given me a note before . . .
. . . or even talked to me,
and she's popular and fashionable. I'd like her to be my friend.
Fashion Kitty thought about the situation and chose her words carefully.
Priscilla Persian is a horrible, spoiled, mean kitty!

And you, Mary Jane Tabby, are a kind, thoughtful, good kitty!!
And maybe just a little too trusting.
Priscilla was playing a trick on you! She wanted you to wear a silly outfit to school so she and her fancy friends could laugh at you.
Shame on her!
Mary Jane started to cry. It's never nice to find out you've been tricked.
Don't cry, Mary Jane. I'm here to help you. Nothing makes a kitty feel better than a Fashion Kitty makeover.
Boohoo! Really?
Mary Jane and Fashion Kitty spent a fantastic hour together.
See, you can wear your hair in cute pigtails, if you want.
Oh, I've always wanted to. But I've been too shy to try.

Fashion Kitty says ...
You can make exciting new looks, right from your closet!
Exciting
New
Mix & Match Fun

Are you sure I can wear these striped stockings with this skirt?
Oh, yes!

Sometimes a kitty just needs a friend to say it.
Isn't it fun to try something new?
It sure is!
It's like having a whole new wardrobe.

Mary Jane couldn't wait to try on everything in her closet.
See, I'm a snow kitty.
Nice frosty look.

This is for swimming.
Uh-huh.

This is my ballet outfit.
Careful, don't trip on that shoe ribbon.
These are my cozy jammies.
Mmmm, toasty!

Of course, Mary Jane didn't want Fashion Kitty to leave. It's always fun to have an expert pay lots of attention to you.

Good luck, Mary Jane!
Thank you, Fashion Kitty!

What about Priscilla and the polka dots?
Don't you worry about her!

Fashion Kitty flew up to Priscilla Persian's bedroom window and climbed in.

Priscilla was a slave to fashion magazines.

OOOHHH!

That means she didn't have her own style.

She just copied whatever she saw.

Fashion Kitty took all Priscilla's unread fashion magazines and drew dark circles around the fashion models' eyes.

It wasn't a nice thing to do, but then, Priscilla wasn't a very nice kitty.

A job well done!!
Hugga, hugga, hugga, hrrrr, hugga . . .

Lana was in the kitchen eating ice cream and smashed cake,
ICE CREAM
and Mother and Father Kittie were looking up superheroes on the Internet,
SUPERHERO:
when Kiki walked in the front door.
Hello?

As soon as Mother and Father Kittie saw her, they asked all the important "W" and "H" questions.

answered Kiki, and she began to cry. Her head hurt, and she wasn't sure she wanted to be a fashion hero.

and then he and Mother Kittie sat with Kiki while she ate ice cream and three pieces of new birthday cake.

She was surprisingly hungry.

Maybe it was the combination of being hit on the head with those fashion magazines
right when you were making your birthday wish,
guessed Mother Kittie.

What did you wish for?
asked Father Kittie.

But Kiki just rubbed her lumpy head and said:

asked Lana, who was standing in the doorway.

sighed M
Kittie.

said Kiki.

This was a very unusual thing for Kiki to say. It wasn't like her to be generous with Lana; but then this had been an unusual day.

Mother and Father Kittie looked at each other

raised their eyebrows.

This is something adults do when they want to say, "Hey, look at that, isn't that nice?" but don't want their children to hear it.

Lana was full of questions and her mouth was full of chocolate cake, but Mother Kittie didn't say anything about chewing with your mouth open. On a normal day she would have.

No . . . not really, it just felt extra tingly.
Sort of like too much of a tickle.

Kiki wasn't sure why she felt she should keep her adventures as Fashion Kitty a secret.

She was too tired to talk about it anyway.

Well, I think it's time for bed,
said Mother Kitti
I think we'll all feel better tomorrow,
said Father Kittie.

said Lana. And with that, the whole family went right to bed without washing their faces or brushing their teeth . . . It was that kind of day.

I've got to make myself a Fashion Kitty costume,

whispered Kiki to Mousie, and she mumbled words like:

stripes

polka dots

and checks

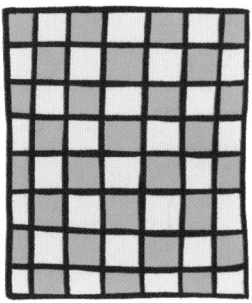

until she fell asleep.

The next morning, while the family was eating breakfast and Kiki was opening her birthday presents from the day before, Kiki said:

said Mother Kittie.

Kiki spent the day trying various costume looks.

Lana, of course, had an opinion about everything.

Kiki didn't pay any attention to her until Lana said:

yelled Kiki. She couldn't help herself. After all, a kitty can only take so much.

Lana looked upset for about five seconds, then she said:

Then she skipped off, singing a song that only a four-year-old would like.

Kiki quickly changed out of the beach-ball outfit, and after only twenty minutes more of fashion work, had a costume she was happy with.

Perfect!
F

asked Mother Kitty, looking at Kiki's flashy new costume. Mothers are always ready for new things, but having your daughter turn into a fashion hero is not one of them.

said Kiki, because she knew it would happen again, and it would be very soon . . .

Epilogue

(which means this is what happened at the end.)

Early the next morning, Priscilla Persian looked at her magazines as soon as she got up.

She picked out her outfit for the day.

After breakfast, Priscilla walked to school.

Everyone is looking at me.
SCHOOL

I must look really good today!

Ha-ha-ha!

I love being me!
Perfect, popular Priscilla! The three P's of me!
Dum de Dum!

Outside, in the school yard, she met her friend Sally.

Priscilla ran screaming into the bathroom.

Boohoo!
Boohoo!
Don't cry, Priscilla. Maybe I can help you.
You will?

Oh, it's you, Mary Jane.
What can you do?
You look, sniff-sniff, nice.
I'll let you borrow my spare glasses for the day. They should cover up your circles.

I guess I'll try.

They work perfectly.

And I think I can see better, too!

Why are you being so nice to me?

I can't help it. I'm just that kind of kitty.

The End

Book Two

Fashion Kitty versus

the Fashion Queen

For my
agent,
Steve, who
is patient,
encouraging,
and yes,
very
fashionable!

This is Kiki Kittie.

And this is Fashion Kitty,
her secret identity.

Kiki Kittie mixes stripes, solids, patterns, and colors with style.

Lana is Kiki's little sister. Lana has her own fashion style.

What? I don't think so.

Who made up this new rule? You?

Sometimes Kiki thinks that Lana is more annoying than other times, and this was definitely one of those "sometimes."

Cassandra? The new kitty at my school? How do you know what Cassandra says?

When someone is catnip purrfect, everyone knows about them.

And then Lana skipped off so fast she didn't hear another word Kiki said.

It is not very satisfying to do lots of arguing first thing in the morning before breakfast.

And it is especially not very satisfying to do lots of arguing with a four-year-old who thinks she is always right.

Kiki tried to smile and make herself feel better, but inside her head she was thinking about the two things she knew about Cassandra . . .

and the one thing she didn't know
but was probably going to find out.

It's not a good thing to decide you don't like someone before you even meet them, but it can happen.

That's her over there. Cassandra, the Fashion Queen.

HMMM.

That's Kiki Kittie. She has a passion for fashion. Just like you!

HMMM

And sometimes once you do meet them it only takes a few words to decide that yes, you were right, you do not like them even one little bit.

Kiki was mad on the outside, sad
wishing for the one thing that w

I wish I could change into Fashion Kitty and teach her a lesson!

It's not easy to keep a super power a secret.
Especially when you'd like to use it to help yourself.

By lunchtime the school was half full of Cassandra clones,

and by three o'clock it was even worse.

Kiki could not believe that someone so new

could become popular so fast.

It was almost like magic.

It was like a kitty having a pet mouse. Or a kitty changing into a fashion superhero. It was unbelievable.

And everyone was talking about it.

Kiki went straight to her room . . .

and slammed the door!

Sometimes, when she is feeling blue, Kiki flips through her Fashion Kitty scrapbook. She has saved every mention Fashion Kitty has ever gotten in the local newspaper.

Kiki was still feeling a little depressed, which is a word that means sad, yucky, and blah all mixed together, when she heard a fashion distress call.

FASHION KITTY!

said Mother, Father, and Lana Kittie all at once when they saw her.

The signal was strong, then weak, then strong, then weak again.

Sounds like someone is having trouble deciding what to wear.

Inside the house that is exactly what was happening.

Does this look OK?

I just can't decide.

Fashion Kitty flew down to the bedroom window and knocked on the glass.
Let me in! Open up! Let me in!
Oh, my gosh! It's you! Fashion Kitty!
And you're Sandy . . . one of Cassandra's new friends.
Oh, yes! Isn't she fabulous? Do you know her?
You're friends with her, aren't you?

Fashion Kitty had to explain the difference between "anti" (which means against) and "auntie" (which is someone who is related to you and hopefully gives you nice presents on your birthday).

Up until two days ago pink was my most favorite color in the whole world.
Uh-huh . . .
I'm wearing my only anti-color outfit!
Everything else in my closet is a little pink, sort of pink, mostly pink, or all pink!

Sandy held up a strange-looking shirt.
I'm coloring in the pink stripes with this black marker, but now the marker is running out of ink, and I'm not even finished! I have two whole stripes left.
Oh, my!
Did you bring some markers? Please say you did!

Fashion Kitty had never met anyone who talked as much as Sandy.

Fashion Kitty paused. Because a fashion hero should mostly try to be kind, even if it is not the easy thing to do.

Fashion Kitty waited, and Sandy waited, and Fashion Kitty waited, and Sandy waited.

Then Fashion Kitty remembered and said:

Fashion Kitty thought carefully about what to say next.

Luckily it landed right in a trash can, because nobody likes a litterbug, even a cute pink one.

When Kiki walked in the front door, Mother, Father, and Lana Kittie said:

all at the same time.

Kiki liked to have some quiet time after a big Fashion Kitty adventure, so the family left her alone to eat her dinner. This was hard for Lana.

After dinner, Kiki went straight to bed.
She knew three things about tomorrow.

Said Kiki to Mousie, and she drifted off to sleep.

It's nice to be right, but somehow not that satisfying if you are right about something bad.

And then Cassandra and her mumbling kitty clones walked off.

But Kiki didn't feel much better, so she guessed that Sandy wasn't feeling much better, either. And she was right.

But as the day went on, Sandy realized she was not as alone as she thought she was. And something happened that surprised even Kiki.

It started with some thinking,

and then some talking,

and then some friendly support,

and finally some doing.

It was a movement in pink.

Almost everyone joined in, even some of the boys.

Kiki could not believe it.

She was overjoyed, which means, happy, happy, happy!

Cassandra could not believe it, either.

She was incensed, which means, mad, mad, mad!

When you have the fashion popularity spotlight all to yourself,

it's not easy to give it up,

even if you don't deserve it anymore.

For days it seemed like all everyone could talk about was Fashion Kitty . . .

Fashion Kitty, and more Fashion Kitty.

Even Kiki was getting a little tired of it.

It's not easy to keep two big secrets from your best kitty friend in the whole world.

Kiki tried not to think about Mousie or Fashion Kitty

as she ate her lunch.

Not far away, someone else was wishing she didn't have to think about Fashion Kitty, either.

And that someone was stamping her foot on the ground,

because that was what she did when she was really

mad.

Cassandra imagined all the ways she could make Fashion Kitty look silly, and all the things she wished she could hear Fashion Kitty say. These imaginings made her smile a very wicked smile.

She didn't know that Fashion Kitty (MOKA* Kiki Kittie) was already suffering, but not quite in the way Cassandra had imagined.

*MOKA
(most often known as)

This was almost too much Fashion Kitty, even for Kiki.

Unfortunately, it did not end well.

Kiki just couldn't help it.

I wouldn't play with you if you begged me!

Sometimes mothers know the exact right thing to say and when to say it.

Mother Kittie could tell that Kiki was having a hard time being a fashion hero, and it would not make things one bit better if she got in trouble for slamming her door.

Across town, Cassandra was up to no good.

Cassandra waited, waited, and waited,

but still no Fashion Kitty.

She didn't know that Fashion Kitty could only respond to real fashion emergencies, and not a fake fashion faux pas.

That night two very different kitties went to sleep with smiles on their lips.

One kitty was right, and the other kitty was wrong. Very wrong!

and on the way to school she made a promise to herself.

She felt very good.

Very good until . . .

WHAT?!

Cassandra is lying! That book is a fake!
Fashion Kitty didn't visit her!
She's a phony!

I can't believe you, Kiki Kittie!
I can't believe how much you hate Fashion Kitty!
But . . .
I don't see how we can stay best friends.

"But" was a big word for Kiki that day.

By the end of the day she felt very angry.

On the way home from school, Kiki thought about all the things that bothered her.

But the thing that bothered her the most was:

And really, if you thought about it, she was right. It wasn't fair at all.

Can we see the book?
Wow.
Here.
Did you see the book?
WOW!
Oh, Cassandra, tell us again what Fashion Kitty was like!
Oh, yes, do.
Maybe later. I want to read to you what it says in here.

Let's see . . . what does it say in *The One and Only Fashion Almanack*?
Look here, it says pink should only be worn on holidays, and then only a little.
Uh-oh. I'm even wearing pink underpants. Does it count if no one can see them?
Wow! That's interesting, isn't it?
Looks like our friend Sandy was wrong. We'll forgive her.
RULES
You can't argue with fashion rules if they are written down.
She's right! If Fashion Kitty wrote it, it must be true.

Cassandra was so happy she skipped all the way home.

And though she didn't look any different, Cassandra certainly seemed to be the Fashion Queen once again.

Can I see the book?
Sorry, Sandy! Don't you think you've done enough damage with your whole pink thing?
You're just lucky that I'm going to forgive you.
Fashion Kitty gave me this book, so it's mine!
FASHION
Am I missing something? Is today a holiday?
No. I just thought pink was okay.
Well, looks like you thought wrong! I'd change my clothes if I were you.

Sometimes Lana was much smarter than a normal four-year-old, and that was what made her special.

The next day, Cassandra was ready for everyone, with some new fashion rules.

Cassandra was using her fashion almanac to make everyone wear exactly what she wanted. She was abusing her fashion power.

Sometimes when a kitty is desperate she might decide to do the wrong thing.

It wasn't a fashion emergency, but it was an emergency for the sake of fashion, and that was good enough.

Sorry, Mother. I have to go. Someone is calling me, and Cassandra needs to be taught a lesson.
Oh, dear! You aren't going to get in a fight, are you?
She's going to beat Cassandra up!

Of course not! No fighting. I promise.
Be careful! At least you've had supper this time.
She's the greatest!

Fashion Kitty flew as fast as she could, and she caught poor Carol Anne by surprise. She was so shocked she broke her necklace by accident.

You didn't? But Cassandra told everyone you did. She said you gave her the almanac.
I did not write that book. It's full of spelling mistakes and . . .
I'm a terrific speller!
It hurts me to say this, but Cassandra is dishonest.
She's a bad kitty!
So I don't have to wear a black hat tomorrow?
No, you don't!!

Both Carol Anne and Fashion Kitty felt a lot better.
Excuse me, Fashion Kitty.
You don't have to raise your hand.
Oh . . . but how is anyone going to believe me?
About meeting you and what you said.
Fashion Kitty thought about it while she fixed Carol Anne's favorite necklace.
One more twist and it's as good as new.
And when it was time to go they had a plan all worked out.
Thank you, Fashion Kitty!
Happy to help!

Fashion Kitty flew home, and she felt as light as an autumn leaf. She looked at all the twinkling lights below her, and even though the air was cold she didn't mind it one bit.

Lana was still up when Kiki walked in the door. She was full of questions.

Sounds like a good story for tomorrow.
Because I know a little kitty who should be in bed.
Do I have to wash my face and brush my teeth?
Come on, Lana. Let's brush them together.
I'm going to go to bed, too.
Tomorrow is going to be a big day.

The next day was a big day. It started off as a big black-hat day.

And then Cassandra spotted Carol Anne.

All the kitties gasped in horror.

Cassandra was happy that everyone was watching her. She was going to make an example out of Carol Anne. She was going to teach her a lesson.

Carol Anne looked nervous, but she took a deep breath and said:

The crowd of kitties started mumbling excitedly.

Cassandra was a little confused. What Carol Anne had said was not what she had expected.

If it had been the olden times she would have said:

But you couldn't really do that kind of thing today, in a modern school yard. Cassandra couldn't think of what to say, so she said:

one more time while her kitty brain tried to think of something clever.

Everyone tried to get a peek at the cover to see if Carol Anne was right.

What Carol Anne said next shocked and excited everyone. It shocked Cassandra so much that she dropped the fashion almanac and ran all the way home.

Everyone wanted to see the photo, and everyone wanted to see the note. The principal put them both on display in the gym for the last two hours of school. They were all way too excited to work anyway.

What's going on?
I don't know.
I'm so sorry! You probably can't forgive me. I was so unfair to you.
Don't cry, June

Of course I can forgive you. I miss you.
You're my best friend!

Must be a friend thing.

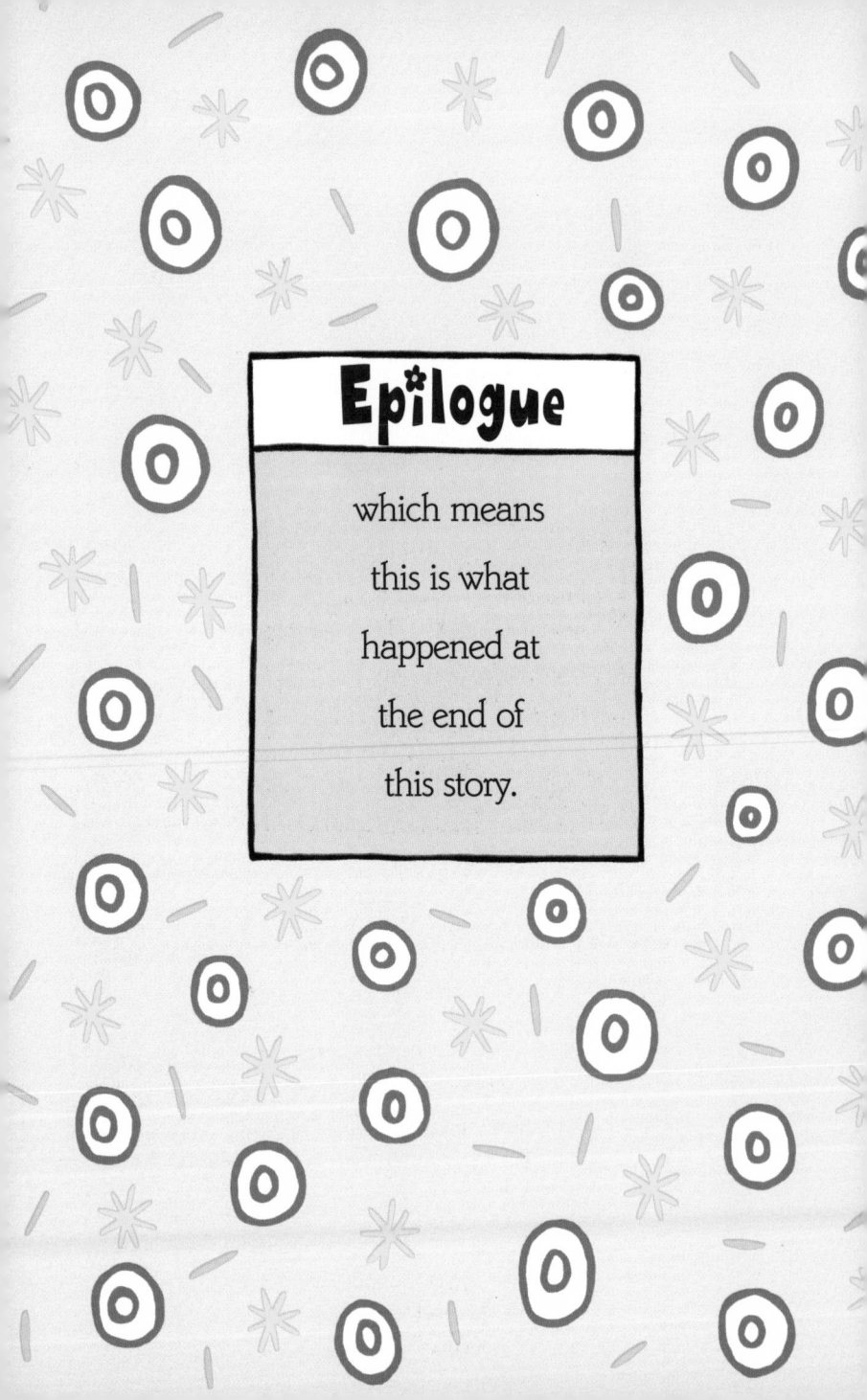

Epilogue

which means
this is what
happened at
the end of
this story.

To show how angry they were with Cassandra, all of the students marched to her house and threw their black hats on her front lawn. It wasn't a nice thing to do, and it wasn't a supermean thing to do, but it was something to do with all the extra black hats that made sense.

Stop sulking, Cassandra! You get out there, young lady, and pick up those hats!
I have to mow the lawn.

STUPID HATS!

The next day when Cassandra went back to school, she pretended like nothing had ever happened.

She was a fantastic actress. The drama teacher heard about her talent and soon had her busy rehearsing for the Thanksgiving play.

She was perfect for the part.

Kiki and June were best friends again, and Kiki was even making a special effort to be nice to Lana.

Thought Kiki Kittie, and that was a very nice thing to be thinking right before falling asleep.

Yes, it is!